THE CAT'S PAJAMAS

For my mother,
Margaret Olive Bunel Edwards de Jourdan (1918–2007),
and for my love, Katie Freeman.

Kids Can Press acknowledges the financial support of the Government of Ontario, through the Ontario Media Development Corporation's Ontario Book Initiative; the Ontario Arts Council; the Canada Council for the Arts; and the Government of Canada, through the BPIDP, for our publishing activity.

Published in Canada by
Kids Can Press Ltd.
29 Birch Avenue
Toronto, ON M4V 1E2

Published in the U.S. by
Kids Can Press Ltd.
2250 Military Road
Tonawanda, NY 14150

www.kidscanpress.com

The paintings in this book were rendered in watercolor, colored pencil and gouache.
The text is set in Bernhard Modern.

Edited by Tara Walker Designed by Karen Powers

This book is smyth sewn casebound.
Manufactured in Tseung Kwan O, Kowloon, Hong Kong, China,
in 3/2010 by Paramount Printing Co. Ltd.

CM 10 09 87 6 5 4 3 2 1

Library and Archives Canada Cataloguing in Publication

Edwards, Wallace
The cat's pajamas / by Wallace Edwards.

ISBN 978-1-55453-308-4 (bound)

1. English language — Idioms — Juvenile literature. I. Title.

PE1460.E47 2010   j428   C2010-900209-1

Kids Can Press is a *Corus*™ Entertainment company

THE CAT'S PAJAMAS

WALLACE EDWARDS

KIDS CAN PRESS

IDIOM: *a group of words whose meaning cannot be understood from the meaning of the individual words; an expression, peculiar to a specific language, that cannot be translated literally*

The more Mr. Katz sewed, the more he got the hang of it.

On the day of his art show, Vincent was so nervous
he didn't know if he was coming or going.

As judge of the Tiny Tot Talent Contest,
Leon had to face the music.

Beryl thought constantly about her big hat collection;
she had a real bee in her bonnet.

The Clothesline Club loved hanging out;
their motto was "birds of a feather flock together."

No matter where he went, Inspector Reinhold
always thought something smelled fishy.

Blanche discovered that finding her way home
from the party was a piece of cake.

As soon as he started his new job, Harold's ears were ringing.

Wade had never driven a submarine before,
so he couldn't wait to get his feet wet.

As much as the Sugar-Bunnies enjoyed traveling,
they were always happy to return to their home sweet home.

Although they frequently disagreed, when it came to staying dry
Foxworth and Featherstone saw eye to eye.

By his second time around on the Happy Hurler,
Hammy was having more fun than a barrel of monkeys.

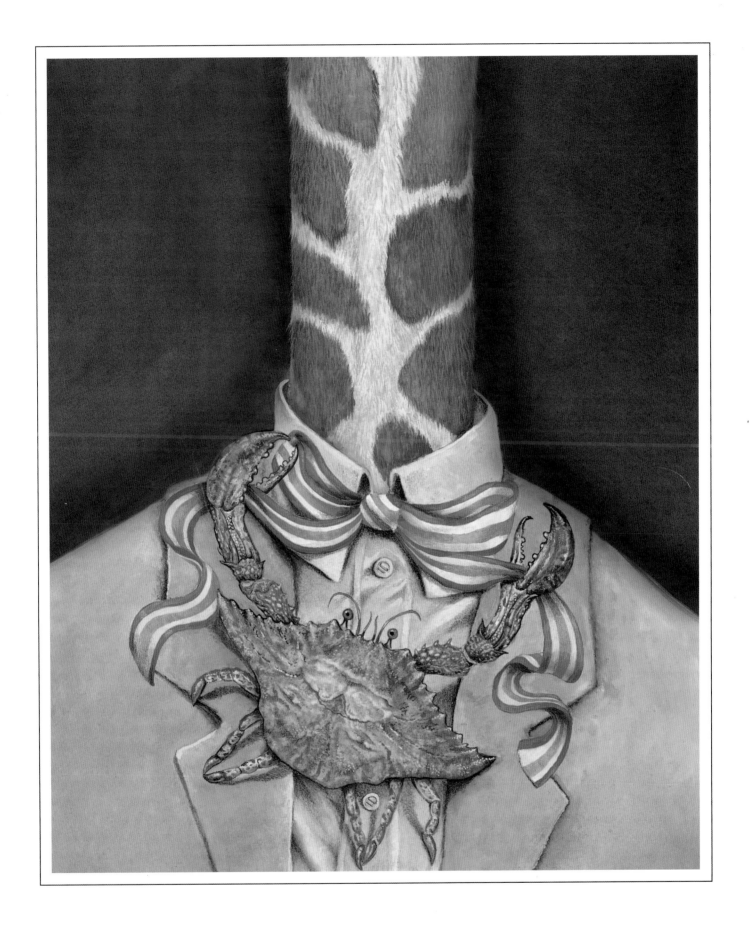

Gerrard was terrible at tying bows, but Claudia
could always be counted on in a pinch.

The Oasis Express was running late, so Camilla had to cool her heels.

The Waddle Rockets finally began to pick up speed
once Little Red got her ducks in a row.

Tina's day was going great ...
until she realized she had a tiger by the tail.

In order to have dinner music, Andy was forced to use his noodle.

Ahab didn't mind if one got away;
he knew there were plenty more fish in the sea.

As expected, Barney graduated with flying colors.

Horace and Shelley sometimes preferred moving at a snail's pace.

After he got a frog in his throat, Big Bill couldn't sing a note.

The sight of Sir William's new painting made Anita hold her tongue.

The great jazz musician Lane Poet liked to blow his own horn.

When it came to cartooning, Elsie had a lot to draw on.

Florence often felt bored surfing, but it was
easier to just go with the flow.

Did you find a hidden cat on each page?

Princess knew that when everything comes together
just so, it's truly the cat's pajamas.

LETTING THE CAT OUT OF THE BAG

Here's what these idioms mean …

A LOT TO DRAW ON: *a great amount of experience or information to use*

BEE IN YOUR BONNET: *a thought or an idea that you are stuck on; an obsession*

BIRDS OF A FEATHER FLOCK TOGETHER: *those who are alike stick together*

BLOW YOUR OWN HORN: *to brag about or praise yourself*

CAT'S PAJAMAS: *someone or something that is excellent or outstanding; this expression is thought to have come from E.B. Katz, an English tailor in the late 1700s and early 1800s, who made fine silk pajamas for royalty and other wealthy clients*

COOL YOUR HEELS: *to be kept waiting*

EARS ARE RINGING: *a ringing sound heard after a loud noise*

FACE THE MUSIC: *to accept the consequences of your actions; to receive punishment*

FROG IN YOUR THROAT: *a hoarseness in the throat that prevents you from speaking clearly*

GET THE HANG OF: *to learn how to do something or to understand something*

GET YOUR DUCKS IN A ROW: *to get organized*

GET YOUR FEET WET: *to do something for the first time*

GO WITH THE FLOW: *to do what others are doing or to agree with others; to go along with or accept what is happening*

HOLD YOUR TONGUE: *to keep silent*

HOME SWEET HOME: *there is no place like home; an expression used when you are glad to be home*

IN A PINCH: *stuck or in need of help*

MORE FUN THAN A BARREL OF MONKEYS: *very funny or enjoyable*

NOT KNOW IF YOU ARE COMING OR GOING: *to be very confused*

PIECE OF CAKE: *something easy*

PLENTY MORE FISH IN THE SEA: *many other possibilities or choices*

SEE EYE TO EYE: *to agree completely with someone or have exactly the same opinion*

SMELLS FISHY: *something that seems dishonest or suspicious*

SNAIL'S PACE: *very slowly*

TIGER BY THE TAIL: *a big problem or something difficult to manage*

USE YOUR NOODLE: *to use your brain; to think*

WITH FLYING COLORS: *easily and very successfully*